Griffinwood Close

Also by J. Lynn Carr

A Werewolf In Mims
Wish You Were Here

Griffinwood Close

J. Lynn Carr

pagethirteen

Second paperback edition May 2024

Book design by J. Lynn Carr

ISBN: 979-8-9882084-6-4 (paperback)

www.pagethirteenpress.com

For every misfit and mischief

Author's Note

I wrote *Griffinwood Close* at a time of upheaval; the first notes for the story began in a hospital waiting room. Writing the story was as healing to me as the the Close is to its residents. I hope this story can do the same for you, dear reader.

This republished edition does not tamper with the story too much, though some parts have been edited for clarity and consistency.

The most notable changes are visual, with a smaller trim size and custom design elements. However, since this story has now gone through even more rounds of editing and proofreading, I have no excuses for any remaining typos, except, perhaps, for the fact that I am human.

Happy reading,
J. Lynn Carr

Part I

Winter

Chapter 1

Emil Jones is losing blood. It gushes from his neck as he drags himself through the forest, the bottom of his boots gummed up with dead leaves.

His breathing is ragged and loud in his ears. The smell of his sweat and blood mingles with the dampness of the night. His hand covers his neck, but it does little to stop the blood. It flows hot and sticky down his arm. He thinks about the beast who tore a chunk from his neck, but his brain reminds him it wasn't a beast but a man.

Just a man with blond hair and tar-black eyes. His teeth may have been predator sharp, his grip like that of a lion grasping onto his dinner, but even delirious with blood loss, Emil thinks that it is not the weapon itself that is evil but how the soldier decides to use it. The man was made a beast by the dogma, evident by the red band around his arm, that courses through his heart, his beliefs as dark as the night sky in the city.

The sky in the forest is different than the sky in the city. It is brighter for one, no longer a coarse black blanket made solid by a permanent fog. Instead, it is a silky, luminescent blue beset with jewels. The earth smells differently here, too. Older, yet freshly turned, with a sense of some impending performance of green.

It is late Winter, he seems to recall, and Spring is knocking on the door.

The trees thin and Emil comes upon a clearing of tall grass turned soft in the moonlight. He is lost, he realizes, with a sinking feeling in his stomach. He doesn't know how much longer he can drag his body forward through the endless night. The dizziness is already setting in, turning the grass into undulating waves.

There is a roaring in his ears, like an ocean wave breaking against the shore—but there is no ocean, or maybe there is and he is the shore. The noise washes over him as he stumbles forward into the field, fighting against the knowledge that he will succumb to the bite in his neck and the venom coursing through his veins.

But then, suddenly, it is no longer a field but a circular courtyard lined with mismatched houses. The entrance is marked by a wrought-iron gate dripping with a passionflower vine. Together, the iron and waxy green tendrils of the vine reach up and over, meeting in the middle above the entryway to form the words "Griffinwood Close."

Beyond the gate, a fountain, crowned by a winged creature, sits in the center of the courtyard. Both eagle and lion are represented in bronze, the sculpture tarnished with age. The air smells sweet, like lilacs and freshly baked bread.

Emil stumbles forward again, toward the fountain, intent on remedying the dryness in his mouth.

He kneels, his hands black with dirt, and clutches the edge of the fountain. His blood smears against the white stone, and he feels a pang of embarrassment. What would his mother think of his manners, getting blood on everything...

He leans forward. He can just make out his reflection in the water, his angular features covered in mud and blood, and something else—a thick black substance that oozed from the soldiers he fought on the battlefield. The tip of his nose just touches the water before he releases a shaky breath and succumbs to the pain.

The peal of the bell signifies an emergency town meeting, and Altair is not happy about this. However, as per Section 2B, Paragraph 1 of the Griffinwood Lease Agreement, he is contractually obliged to attend any and all town meetings, regardless of the hour.

So he tosses back his quilt and ties his robe around his waist before stalking, quite angrily, out of Number Two and into the courtyard. His mouth is open, about to spew forth a selection of complaints, when the smell of blood hits him like a wall, and he closes his mouth quickly, clenching his jaw against the tightness in his gums.

His teeth sharpen into fine points when he sees the body crumpled beside the fountain, a hunter's instinct awakening deep in his bones. His mouth waters, trying to convince him that he is thirsty, though he shouldn't be after his dinner an hour earlier. He can smell the earthiness of the person—a heady mix of musk and green grass and something a little floral, like orange blossoms. Underneath, however, is the scent of blood-soaked earth, broken wood, and a hint of decay.

Whoever it is, they are very close to death.

Altair's neighbor, Mrs. Flint of Number Three, is leaning over the body, still ringing the bell.

"Yes," he says. "We hear you."

Mrs. Flint jumps slightly, giving him a confused look. Then, her bright red eyes float down to her arm, which is still ringing the bell as if of its own accord. "Oh, dear," she says, lowering her arm. She turns the bell upside down and holds it by the clapper, her long nails scratching briefly against the metal. Her lower jaw juts forward, showing her pointy teeth, and she furrows her brow in worry, clutching her nightgown tighter around her chest.

As a redcap, she should be wearing the knitted hat that she would have received at birth and subsequently soaked in the blood of those she would have been expected to kill. However, Mrs. Flint didn't have the stomach for violence, despite her genetic inheritance, and Altair has only seen her wear her cap once, when she stumbled into Griffinwood looking confused and bleary-eyed. It was a faded pink, so faint that he could tell immediately she only had one death on her hands (a significant amount less than a redcap at her age should have accumulated).

"So sorry, Altair," she says, "but I wasn't sure what to do. I heard him cross under the arch." She gestures vaguely toward the entryway. There is a trail of blood that leads out beyond the fence and into the forest beyond.

The forest is a lie, however. Griffinwood Close does not exist in the middle of a forest, or, indeed, in the middle of anywhere. As an entirely self-sufficient pocket of reality that reveals itself to whomever it feels it can help, it just *is*.

Altair looks down at their unexpected arrival: a young man clearly in need of refuge. He is on his side, a lock of hair covering his face. He wears a military uniform, though because of the peculiarities of Griffinwood's existence, the soldier could be from any number of places, eras, or dimensions, and Altair isn't able to determine what kind of military uniform it is. There is something in the manner of design, however, that makes him think the soldier is from his own world, though certainly from a later time than Altair.

"I pulled him out of the fountain," says Mrs. Flint, "to check for a pulse. He's still alive."

A large wound marks the man's neck, dark and clotted with blood. It's a wonder he's still alive.

Altair nods. "I can hear a heartbeat, but it is faint and fading fast."

By now, the Close is awake, porch lights flickering on as the residents, so rudely called away from potential slumber, file out of their homes, pulling on sweaters and robes and rubbing their eyes. They gather around the fallen soldier, their faces lit by the unearthly glow of the false moon above.

Briar Fernbug and his roommate, Markos (last name unknown), from Number Four, stand on the other side of Mrs. Flint.

"What is it?" asks Briar. His hooves

nervously clop against the cobblestone, and he reaches up to touch the tip of one of his horns that curls back from his forehead and around his ear—a nervous habit that is common among fauns, similar to how pixies chew their nails down to the quick or how hobgoblins twist their stolen rings around their spindly fingers. Briar was brutally punished and subsequently cast out of his village for accidentally stepping on the robe of an elvish dignitary, and, since then, he is often in a state of worry that he has either offended someone or accidentally hurt them in some way.

Post-Traumatic Stress Disorder, as a book in Altair's library defined it.

Markos frowns and raises his gloved hands, signing an answer. "A man."

Although Markos's voice was stolen before he was born, his touch was stolen by a witch much later in life. Gifted as he is with his own magic, he has never been able to find a counter-curse to the cruel punishment enacted on him when he was a foolish boy, too ready to kiss and lie.

The witch's curse ensures that everything Markos touches eventually withers, including the gloves he wears. He typically gets two weeks of use out of a pair of gloves before the edges fray and the stitches come loose. A sewing circle (mandatory as per Section 3A, Paragraph 5 of the Griffinwood Lease Agreement) ensures Markos will always have a new pair of gloves. Altair makes a mental note that his right-hand glove is due soon.

"What should we do?" asks Mrs. Flint.

"We'll need Dawn," says Altair, looking for the red-haired witch who lives in Number Five.

Dawn Abberton steps forward with her wand raised. "I'm here." She and her son, Henry, are the newest residents of Griffinwood Close, chased here by hellhounds intent on killing Henry, the heir to the throne of the Underworld. Dawn had no idea that the man she had fallen in love with was a demon, let alone a high-ranking official who was at the forefront of a coup against whoever was in charge of the Underworld at the time. Altair could never keep track, to be frank. "Please step back. I'll need to cast some diagnostic spells to get an idea of what's wrong."

Altair snorts. "We can tell what's wrong. It's the man's neck. He's been bitten."

"Bitten by what?" asks Dawn's son, pushing through to stand next to his mother. When they first moved to Griffinwood Close, Henry was barely up to his mother's hip. Now the boy is almost as tall as his mother, who is a head shorter than Altair. Two horns have just broken through the skin on his forehead, and his leathery wings are tucked close behind him. His fourteenth birthday is next Autumn, and Altair has had the misfortune of being selected for the Party Planning Committee.

"A vampire," says a soft voice behind the group.

Altair turns, though he knows what he will see before he does: a fae leaning on a cane of twisted, knotted oak. Her wings are large and paper-thin, resembling wrinkled leaves falling to the earth between seasons. They stand so tall off her back that he can see the pale globe of the moon through them.

Her arms are lined with thorns, and her head is covered with rose petals, curling around her pointed ears and resting against the collar of her nightgown. Her waxy green tendrils of hair fall around her shoulders and cascade down her back.

Her body is slim and youthful, but her

shoulders droop with age, weighed down by the necklace of walnut shells around her throat that stores her memories.

Arabella Twigs lives in Number One, and, although she is not the founder of Griffinwood Close, she has called the Close home far longer than any of her neighbors. She looks up at Altair. "But you knew that, didn't you?"

He nods. "I can smell it."

"Indeed," she says, her eyes crinkling in approval. "It's not just the smell of a vampire you detect, though, is it?" Arabella looks up at him beneath dew-lined eyelashes.

"No," he admits. "It's a particular vampire." He is aware of his neighbors' gaze as he looks down at the wounded soldier and sighs. "It's him. It's Valentine."

The name falls from his lips, and he imagines it landing on the ground in front of him to seep in between the cobblestones, putrefying the earth below. A befitting image to represent Valentine, leader of a sect of vampires whose sole endeavor is shedding human blood while causing the most amount of pain and chaos possible.

Valentine was a ruthless ruler, though,

admittedly, not as ruthless as Altair had once been. The smell of rot and copper comes to him unbidden, and his throat bobs in unfelt emotion, recalling the particular sound of mortal screams, throaty with despair.

Arabella is still looking at him curiously. They all are, he realizes with some alarm, as if waiting for the answer to a question she hasn't asked yet.

When Altair arrived at Griffinwood Close, he was half-mad with despair. He still remembers the feeling, like a hole torn in his chest. That Valentine could reach him here— in the safe refuge absconded from both time and space existing in some sliver between universes—is almost unfathomable. And yet, the thought is equally inevitable, as resolute as a bogie's ability to fall for the simplest of lies.

Altair feels no better than a bogie at the moment. He had, indeed, been trying to trick himself into thinking that Valentine had long since forgiven his transgressions, or perhaps even forgotten him altogether. With the arrival of this unexpected neighbor and his rapidly healing vampire bite that smells of copper and tree bark decaying in the damp,

Altair wonders if this is a message for him. At the very least, he doubts this is a coincidence, having, quite some time ago, decided that coincidences are always lies.

Yet the sinking fear in his stomach is not for himself but for his neighbors, who welcomed him to Griffinwood Close with open arms and have worked diligently without complaint to accommodate his dietary requirements and make him feel welcome and appreciated.

"He can't track him here," he says, much more confidently than he feels, "unless there is something of his—something with which he carries a bond—to help him detect the border. Bonds are intentional. This bite is savage, the likely result of battle. He might not have even meant to turn him. Otherwise, Griffinwood Close will remain hidden, only revealed to those in need. And I highly doubt Valentine is in need."

It is speculation at best, but his neighbors accept his reasoning with curt nods, including Arabella, who purses her lips in agreement at this answer.

Arabella looks at the young soldier and then up at the griffin sculpture crowning the fountain. "Our esteemed guardian has selected a new resident for us, it would seem."

Number Five, with its white-washed facade and wrap-around porch adorned in lilac bushes poised to bloom at any second, is the largest and tallest home on Griffinwood Close. Dawn's rooms are on the first floor, while Henry has taken over the attic. He is often seen on the roof, reading or working on an essay assigned by one of his neighbors, who act as professors in the absence of a more traditional schooling structure.

The second floor contains a guest bedroom with a twin-size bed in a tarnished gold frame, made up neatly with a handmade quilt from Mrs. Flint. Altair carries the soldier's body, so cold in his arms, and gently places him onto the bed. It is next to the window overlooking the courtyard, and Altair glances down briefly at the fountain, wondering, not for the first time, about the inner mechanics of Griffinwood Close and the unique magical construct that holds it in place. He has the impression that the griffin is smirking at him, and, perhaps this isn't a message from Valentine but a decision made by the mischief of this land. He has the sinking feeling that they are merely falling prey to the machinations of forces beyond their understanding.

Altair steps back to allow Dawn to examine her patient. He watches as she raises her wands and chants words under her breath. Altair doesn't recognize the language. It sounds vaguely like Latin, though it is not a dialect with which he is familiar.

"Can you take it away?" he asks Dawn quietly.

Her eyes are bright with understanding. "I'm sorry," she says softly. "It doesn't work that way. I can only facilitate his healing. The bite has already tainted his blood. The transition into a vampire has begun."

He nods.

"But perhaps it isn't so bad?" she says, cautiously. She looks down at their new neighbor, using her free hand to brush back a lock of his hair. "We have two new calves and more than enough goats. I'm sure they can handle a few extra blood draws here and there. You're the only other vampire, and I'm sure...? Perhaps it would be nice to have someone else around? Someone who can understand...?"

He sighs, hearing the silent entreaty in between her stuttering sentences. Altair is not as social as his neighbors would prefer. And while they do not judge him for his moods or his need to sequester himself inside his house from time to time, he knows they worry. He can see the brow lines and worried glances—the small looks of concern that annoy him as much as they warm his heart. "I don't need someone to understand. The only thing I need is peace and quiet."

Chapter 2

Emil wakes to the sound of a teacup shattering against the hardwood floor.

"Oh dear," says a voice. "I'm so sorry, Markos. Did I get any tea on you?"

Emil opens his eyes to see a man kneeling down to clean his spilled tea, his gloved hands carefully collecting the broken bits of ceramic and placing them in a trash receptacle. The man sitting beside him is clutching the collar of his shirt nervously. "Thank you, Markos. That's so kind of you," he says, and Emil realizes that the voice he heard belongs to this man, whose legs are short, hairy, and hooved.

He recalls an illustration from one of his childhood books, a retelling of Greek myths, and he recognizes the man as a faun. He has never seen a faun in real life before—he didn't really think they existed, to be frank—but he also didn't believe the monsters he encountered on the battlefield were real either. Their sharp teeth, unnaturally colored eyes, and the fact that they could take several bullets or hatchet wounds before they succumbed to the inevitability that is death have prepared him to believe the unbelievable.

Markos nods at his companion kindly and moves his hands in a series of movements that the faun seems to understand.

"I know," replies the faun with a sheepish smile. "Always so clumsy. Where would I be without you to help me keep myself together?"

Markos signs something that makes the faun laugh. Emil shifts, and the sound catches the attention of the two.

"He's awake!" squeaks the faun. "Markos, will you let Dawn know? Oh, don't try to sit up. You've had an accident."

The faun moves closer to Emil and places a cool hand on his arm, which is when Emil realizes that his neck and shoulder have been bandaged in pristine white gauze.

"My name is Briar," says the faun. "Would you like some water?"

Emil introduces himself to Briar, his voice stuttering over his official title so much so that he decides to forgo it. He's fairly certain he no longer has an army to fight for anyway. The faun helps him lean forward to grasp the glass of water with his mouth. "Thank you," he says.

When Markos returns, it is with a young, red-haired woman. Although he doesn't recognize the wooden stick as any particular type of medical instrument, he recognizes the swift efficiency of her movements as she checks his bandages, her hands cool and supple. A nurse, he thinks. He must be in a medical facility.

She introduces herself as Dawn and explains that they found him in the courtyard, face down in the fountain, bleeding profusely from what looks like a bite on his neck. He feels it fully now—the fire in his throat, the fatigue in his limbs.

"The monster who... who did this to me..."

Dawn makes a hushing sound that reminds him of his mother. "You need more sleep," she says, and with a wave of her wooden stick, a honey-soft warmth washes over his eyelids, dragging them downward.

He awakes again a few hours later. There is a different man sitting in the chair. He leans back casually, his legs crossed at the ankle, reading a slim paperback. His clothes are at least a century out of date, but there is an effortless elegance to the man that he finds curious.

Emil watches as the man's frown deepens and he turns the page in his book, intent upon some plot device that has suddenly revealed itself. He leans forward then, his elbows on his knees, and shakes his head.

"What are you reading?"

Emil's voice sounds loud in his ears; indeed, it must be the same for the man because he jumps and nearly drops the book.

He recovers with surprising speed, folding down the corner of the page to mark his place before looking at Emil with pale, golden eyes. "I'll go fetch Dawn," he says. There is a slight accent in his deep, melodic voice that Emil can't quite place, and he glimpses canine teeth that are just a little too long to be human.

He thinks briefly of the monster who held him in a bruising grip as he ripped his life from his throat. Yet, this man, with his pressed trousers, embroidered waistcoat, and soft amber eyes, looks nothing like the monster his teeth would have him appear to be.

Before Emil can reply, the man has left the room. He can hear the vague sounds of people moving throughout the house, quick footsteps going down the stairs and muffled voices. He looks around the room, appreciating the warmth of the afternoon sun and the blue expanse of sky beyond.

When Dawn comes back in, the man stands in the doorway, the paperback under his arm. "Well, I'll be off then," he says to Dawn. He gives them both a curt nod and then turns on his heel, leaving Emil with the sense that he has been dismissed in some way, like a child being shooed away from the headmaster's office.

Dawn smiles and sits down on the edge of the bed. It creaks underneath her weight, the patched quilt tightening around his legs as she leans forward to look at his bandage. "You'll have to forgive Altair. He doesn't do well with change, and you... well, you're a bit of a surprise for us all here."

"I'm so sorry," he says reflexively. "I

didn't mean to intrude."

She furrows her brow in mock annoyance. "Oh, don't you start," she says, her deft fingers teasing the space around his injuries, searching for infection. "The Griffinwood defenses don't part unless they trust someone. You are perfectly welcome here."

"Tell me more," he asks. It sounds glib to his ears, but he is unsure how to continue the conversation. Indeed, his mind is filled with unanswered questions, and he doesn't know how to disentangle them from the memory of battle, from the smell of dirt and blood, from the soreness in his neck, and from the burning in his throat.

Dawn tells him that Griffinwood Close is a home. It exists outside of the world Emil knows and is only accessible to those it deems worthy or in need of something it feels it can give.

"So, it's a sentient thing, this place?"

Dawn weighs the question in her head, her mouth twisted to the side in contemplation. "Perhaps. No one really knows. Arabella has been here almost her entire life and still doesn't really know how this place works. You'll meet her soon, I'm sure." She pauses, looking down at him curiously. "Are you experiencing any peculiar cravings? Having any violent thoughts?"

"My injuries are a result of a vampire bite," he says quietly as if he has just remembered the words. "What you're really asking is how far into the transition I am, yes?"

"How much do you know about vampires?"

"I know enough. They are not common where I'm from, but there was a small group of them to the east of where I was stationed. They attacked my company. I saw a few of my friends turned, before I..." He pauses, looking out of the window as if he can see his memories projected on the glass. "I don't know if anyone else survived."

He recalls the feeling of teeth sinking into his flesh and remembers that he's not the only one who lost something. He can feel the weight of the gold necklace in his pocket, the chain having snapped as he tried desperately to extract himself from his attacker's embrace. Without thought, he stuffed it into his jacket and ran, taking off directionlessly into the woods. What was it the vampire had said as he stumbled away, his shoulder already wet with blood?

Run, little rabbit.

He shivers, the sunlight no longer pleasantly warm but a harsh, cold spotlight giving away his hiding place. He knows without a doubt that the vampire will come looking for him soon. Will these so-called defenses hold?

Dawn misunderstands the shiver and presses her hand to his forehead. "You're not feverish," she says. "That's a good sign. Do you think you are able to get up out of bed?"

He nods, and she grips his arm to help him stand up. Bare feet planted firmly on the hardwood floor, a wave of nausea washes over him, and he grips his stomach with a grimace.

Suddenly he doesn't feel quite himself, or, at least, his body doesn't feel like his own. Perhaps his mind has relinquished control to some foreign entity flowing through his veins. Or maybe he is dreaming, his joints slowly disconnecting, his limbs floating away from him. He is an unmoored boat, wandering aimlessly among the waves. He blinks, and suddenly he can hear Dawn's heartbeat, so very loud in his head, pulsing, pulsing, pulsing, like a physical thing inside of his temples.

Saliva rushes into his mouth, and his gums are tight and uncomfortable. He clamps his lips together, hoping that he isn't going to vomit, but he feels a sharp pain in his tongue, and his mouth is filled with the warm, metallic taste of his blood.

It tastes delicious, a gilded mix that makes his stomach pang with hunger.

He wants more.

Dawn's hand is still on his arm. Without thinking, he covers it with his own and pushes her body against the wall. His mouth is on her neck, and she smells heavenly, all lilacs and honey and something distinctly alive.

Her blood coating his tongue is even better.

It rushes over his senses like a breeze of cool air in the middle of Summer, and he thinks he could drink her up for the rest of eternity, feel her body pressed against his, and her heartbeat in his mouth, for a lifetime and then some.

Suddenly, there is a loud crack, and a sharp pain spreads through his neck. His body crumples to the floor as he loses consciousness.

Chapter 3

"It's dangerous, having him here," says Mrs. Flint. "If you hadn't snapped his neck, Altair..." She lets the sentence linger in the air and looks around the room.

The town meeting is being held in Arabella's sitting room, which is actually the conservatory, with paned glass walls and a ceiling that affords a full view of the sunset beyond. The room is crowded with plant life, twisting over the floor until no more tile can be seen. There is tea on the table, along with a selection of pastries. Mrs. Flint takes a bite of her blueberry scone and looks meaningfully at Altair.

Altair's focus is on the book in front of him, but his mind is still swirling with what instinct led him to linger on the threshold of Number Five. When the smell of blood and the soft, choked sigh of Dawn reached him, he found himself running up the stairs with a swiftness he had forgotten.

"I agree," says Briar. He stands up, his hooves silent against the fuzzy vines, and selects a pastry for himself. "A youngling vampire is impulsive. He puts us all at risk. Not to mention, he was bitten by Altair's former...friend. I know you think the defenses will hold, but what if this is a trap?"

Altair has returned his attention to his book, but he hasn't read any of the words for quite some time. He can feel their gazes on him, and he merely shrugs, as if disinterested in the reappearance of Valentine in his life.

In reality, if he still had a heartbeat, it would be frantic.

Dawn shakes her head, the movement bringing Altair's eyes to the small square bandage on her neck. Altair's timely arrival, coupled with Emil's youthful clumsiness, resulted in minimal damage. There probably won't even be a bruise. "He didn't know what he was doing. His body is going through changes he doesn't fully understand. He just needs to learn how to handle his new circumstances."

Her cheeks flush lightly as she looks over at her son, who is sitting next to her on the bench, his shoulders slumped forward in the habitual sullenness of a teenager. His attention is on a handheld device with a small screen and buttons he presses in quick succession. Tinny whooshes, cracks, and pows can be heard in the silence.

Arabella nods. "Thank you for reminding us that everyone deserves empathy, Dawn. Altair's suggestion that Griffinwood will remain hidden despite this coincidental connection with Altair is a very reasonable assumption. Griffinwood brought him here, to us, and I trust that this is where he needs to be."

"What do you think, Altair?" signs Markos.

"I think," he begins, folding the corner of the page and closing his book before shifting his chair to look at his neighbors. "It is a common mistake for a youngling vampire to make. I admit that I had hoped the transition would take longer. I did not anticipate an incident like this occurring so soon after his bite."

"What should we do?" asks Briar, leaning forward to look at Altair.

Altair is keenly aware of the dangers of a youngling vampire. Uncontrollable rages, insatiable hunger, untold strength, and quickened healing make them almost impossible to subdue when they inevitably lose control.

He looks at his neighbors, noticing for the first time how fragile their necks look.

He sighs, resisting the urge to rake his fingers through his hair. "Perhaps he will be better able to understand his transition if he resides with me."

He had expected the look he is now receiving from his neighbors—a subtle, shocked look at the fact that Altair would even entertain the idea of having a roommate, let alone be the one to suggest it in the first place. "I will be able to keep a close eye on him," he adds reasonably. "I will act as a safety precaution until he is able to handle his cravings. Until then, I will be his constant companion."

Arabella's smile is soft, and, for a brief second, Altair thinks he sees something spark in her eyes, a flash of thought made visible by its strength and veracity. "It is decided then. We will move our new neighbor to Number Two."

Part 2

Spring

Chapter 4

Although Number Two is one of the smaller houses on the Close, it does, remarkably, have a second bedroom.

As cramped as it is, the spare bedroom, right next to the primary bedroom, has a full-size bed, an armoire, and a small writing desk. Above the desk is a large window, and the morning light slanting through frames Emil's face as he looks at himself in the mirror affixed to the inside of the armoire door.

He presses his thumb to his canine tooth and winces as a tiny drop of blood beads upon his skin. Altair had told him that they will dull over time, forming a point only when he needs to eat. He thinks about Dawn and the feeling of her flesh breaking against his mouth, and he is struck with guilt, despite her assurances that she wasn't upset or permanently harmed by his actions.

His transition happened while he slept, held just away from consciousness by the magic in Dawn's wand and words, but he is not surprised to learn that he is one of the monsters he fought against just a few weeks ago. He has a name now for the vampire who bit him, too—Valentine—and knows that he has a connection to Altair.

When he had finally been allowed to retain consciousness, he wondered idly how to offer himself up to death, but Altair, knowing the contemplative look remarkably well, insisted that wouldn't be necessary. "You'll be perfectly capable of not harming someone with a little bit of practice. Besides," he had added, "we have plenty of livestock, so neither one of us has to starve."

Not starving is crucial, as Altair is constantly reminding him. Regular intake of proper nutrients means sustainable control over instincts that would otherwise see him tearing into everyone's throats. "I won't let that happen," Altair said, quietly but firmly.

Even with Altair's reassurance, Emil promises himself that if he ever bites another person again, he will remove himself from the Close via whatever means are necessary.

He looks out the window at the courtyard below, and for the first time since he stumbled through the gateway, he is able to take in his new surroundings, noting the fountain in the center of the courtyard and the forest beyond. Altair explained that the forest isn't real but that the gardens and stables that lie behind the houses are real enough, providing the residents with plenty of food and natural resources that keep their community afloat. Like the forest, however, the sun overhead is false too, which is why Emil can revel in its warmth instead of suffering the agonizing burns he would otherwise feel.

Altair pointed out each house, telling him the names of the residents. Arabella Twigs in Number One, Mrs. Flint in Number Three, Briar Fernbug and Markos in Number Four, and Dawn and Henry Abberton in Number Five.

Number Six is vacant, and it stands closest to the entryway, casting an irregularly shaped shadow over the wrought-iron gate.

Everyone pitches in, as Altair told him, and Emil knows he will be called upon to do the same soon enough. He is more than ready to get started, feeling his hunger as a buzzing anxiety in his joints. He is desperate for a distraction.

"But first, we will practice self-control," Altair told him. "We will ease into social gatherings." He paused then, giving him a sideways look. "Though, I want to be clear that no one here fears you."

Emil can't help but question that statement. Still, he dresses in the borrowed clothing Altair has laid out for him and makes his way downstairs.

He finds Altair in the sitting room, absorbed in the same paperback he had been reading earlier.

"Must be a good book," Emil says with a soft smile, stuffing his hands in the pockets of his trousers. Despite the fact that the clothes fit remarkably well, he has spent too many years in a uniform and feels awkward without his olive drab coat and his thick-soled boots, covered in mud.

Altair looks up, his eyebrows raised with an unreadable emotion. "Yes," he says, setting the book down on the table beside him. "Now, how are your sewing skills?"

It is still early morning, drops of dew turning the courtyard into a diamond-encrusted lake of slick stone, and Emil curses, his voice carrying through the open window and startling a flock of pixies that were sleeping in the bush outside of Number Four. They shoot up into the air like a rainbow and settle themselves in a tree, far away from the frustration that radiates off Emil's body like a heat wave.

"It's ok. We'll just have to pull out a few stitches and start again," says Briar.

Emil looks at his failed attempt at a glove and sighs, running his hand through his hair. "Thank you for being so patient, Briar. I'm ok at patching holes in socks, but I've never made anything so complicated."

Briar waves his hand dismissively. "It just takes time."

Emil nods and continues again, keenly aware of Altair's gaze lingering on him as he does so. Following Briar's instructions proves harder than anticipated, and his attention is drawn constantly to things beyond their small circle in the sitting room of Number

Four: the morning sun pooling around them from the open window and how it feels so tender against his skin; the sound of Henry practicing his violin next door; the smell of Arabella's famous blueberry scones drawing the attention of the previously displaced flock of pixies, who are chirping in anticipation.

But when Briar pricks his thumb with a needle, the smell of blood washes over him, and he takes a deep breath against the dizziness that spreads through his body. Briar's blood smells like fresh-cut daffodils, vanilla beans in cream, and oak moss.

He feels Altair's gaze intent upon his every move, waiting for the inevitable twitch of a muscle or snarl of a lip. Emil takes another deep breath, letting the sensation wash over him and away, envisioning a pile of leaves scattering in the wind. Altair's readiness proves to be the steady hand he needs, and, following the analogy he has inadvertently summoned, he lets this knowledge take root against his sternum, replacing the leaves of hunger.

"I'll be right back," says Briar. "I'm just going to get a plaster for my thumb."

"That was good," says Altair.

When Emil looks up, Altair's attention is still on his half-made glove, but there is a wisp of approval on his face.

The blood looks heavenly in the wine glass, all rich and thick, coating the sides of the glass in a film of brownish red. Emil holds in a groan of frustration as Altair holds the glass in front of him, just out of reach.

They are in the kitchen of Number Two, the checkered floor gleaming in the afternoon sun pouring through the windows. There is a door that leads to a small patio with a wrought-iron table and mismatched chairs. Beyond the patio, Emil can see glimpses of green and yellow, hints of purple flowers, and trees with fruit ready to be plucked from their boughs.

"Now," begins Altair, "this is the most important lesson I could teach you. I'm sure you are already aware of the power we, as vampires, possess. A preternatural sense of smell, sight, and hearing. An unusual strength courses through our bodies. We are predators without a heartbeat. We do, however, have a heart." He looks at Emil fully now, his eyes soft, his full lips quirked just to the right and upward in as close to a smile as Emil has seen on his face since waking up in Griffinwood Close. "Remember that, please. It is so easy to forget. We are entirely capable of emotions that are not bloodlust—nay, that are the opposite of bloodlust. And while we may be manacled to the most unholy of dietary requirements, we are—and I can't emphasize this enough, Emil—not monsters."

Altair pauses, his expression strained, before arranging his features into a natural impassivity. He places the glass down in front of Emil. "And now, we will sip our drinks. We never gulp. It will only lead to wanting more."

This blood is far less complex than Dawn's, but the hunger in his veins is subdued just as well. "Is it different when it comes directly from the source? Or from an animal instead of...?"

Altair dabs his lips with a cotton napkin. "Yes, blood extracted and stored will always lose something of its essence. But it is just as nourishing. We take only what we need from the livestock and store it using a stasis spell that I helped develop with Dawn.”

“Do you always consume meals here, in the kitchen?”

He nods. “Or in the formal dining room.”

“What about the patio?”

“Pardon?”

Emil smiles and motions toward the door. “We could sit on the patio. The weather is nice enough.”

Altair frowns, attempts to form a rebuttal to this suggestion, and yet finds none that seems worthy of gracing his lips. “I suppose so.”

This is how Arabella finds them. Altair sits straight-backed in the chair but, to his credit, has rolled his sleeves up to reveal surprisingly pale, slender wrists. She can just make out the jagged line of a scar that runs along his right forearm—a result of a fight with a werewolf centuries ago. He grips his glass tightly but swirls its contents around languidly, pausing to savor its aroma before taking a tight-lipped, calculated sip.

Emil lounges in the chair, his shirt untucked and sleeves rolled up to his elbows. His legs are crossed casually, and he sips his blood with a laugh. “Altair, that can’t be true," he is saying. "I'm sure you were a wonderful Juliet in Briar's adaptation of *Romeo and Juliet.*"

Altair replies, but Arabella doesn't catch his words. She has already turned to walk away, a smile playing on her rosy lips. She can't even remember what brought her over here, but it wasn't so urgent anyway.

Chapter 5

The gardens that circle Griffinwood Close fill the air with the verdant smells of Spring.

There is a distant sound of chickens clucking and the bell of a dairy cow wandering aimlessly through the field. The flock of pixies has made their way to the orange grove, and they feast on fallen fruit, their brightly colored bellies full and happy.

Today, Altair and Emil are harvesting peas. They work in companionable silence, moving along the trellis and depositing their peas in a basket on the ground between them.

"I hated peas when I was a kid," says Emil, dropping the offensive green legume into the basket.

Altair smirks. "Well, you won't have to worry about eating them anymore."

Emil nods and tosses another pea. He looks

at Altair, whose movements are effortlessly graceful and yet efficient. Emil still feels like a scrawny schoolchild standing next to him, even more so in his borrowed clothes.

Today, he is wearing a pair of linen trousers and a thin white shirt. He's left the top three buttons undone and rolled his sleeves up to his elbows. He feels unkempt next to Altair's full-buttoned shirt with a navy tie, navy waistcoat, and matching pants. Good lord, the man even has silver cufflinks. Who wears cufflinks while harvesting peas?

A centuries-old vampire, it would seem.

Yesterday, while they lounged on the patio and felt the sun slant downward toward the fields beyond, Emil asked Altair how long he had been living at Number Two, Griffinwood Close. Altair had given him a vague answer—something like, "A while now"—but surprisingly, he followed it up with his age. "Though I have been in this state of interminable damnation for seven centuries."

Altair seemed just as taken aback by his willingness to share this information as Emil was to receive it, and Altair retired to his rooms shortly after. "I must finish this abomination of a book for book club next week."

Emil snaps a pea off the vine and lets it fall into the basket. A shadow passes, and he looks up to see Markos walking by. Markos gives them a nod and continues walking toward the chicken coop, an ax slung over his shoulder.

Emil turns back to Altair and observes his profile—the long, angular nose, the high cheekbones, the lock of dark, curled hair that has fallen across his forehead. His dark skin is lined in gold from the morning sun.

"What was your favorite meal as a child?" asks Emil.

Altair pauses, taken aback by the question. He hasn't thought of his childhood in centuries. Suddenly, he can hear the pops and sizzles of oil over heat and feel the stickiness of dates dripping in honey against his fingertips. Briefly, he recalls the sensation of his mouth watering for some long-forgotten treat. The word comes to him out of the depths of his forgotten memory. "Zulabiyya."

He describes it to Emil, who nods knowingly. "Like a doughnut."

Altair laughs lightly, dropping another pea into the basket. "If you say so."

"Do you think you have a recipe in that dusty library of yours?" He had caught a glimpse of the library yesterday, a wood-paneled room lined with rows and rows of books with tattered, well-loved leather covers. It wasn't dusty (quite the opposite, in fact) but he is amused by the sudden, stricken look Altair gives him.

"Perhaps," he says warily.

Emil smirks and turns back to the trellis, but the scent of blood overtakes the smell of dirt and leaves around them, and he can no longer focus on the task before him.

Altair notices the smell, too, and whips around to find the source. "It's Markos," he says. "Preparing a chicken for dinner, I think."

But when Altair turns back to Emil, he is no longer there.

Altair finds Emil outside the barn. He stands in the doorway, hands clenched in white-knuckled fists. "Emil."

His voice is soft, but Emil jumps just the same, and when he turns to look at Altair, his eyes have gone dark, shielded in red. His canine teeth are razor-sharp.

"Emil." Altair takes a step forward, his hands held in front of him as if approaching a feral animal. "Let's go inside and leave Markos to his task."

Altair chances a glance beyond Emil and can see Markos watching them intently, the ax gripped tightly in his hand. He inclines his head toward the ax. Altair shakes his head, a silent affirmation that the ax will not be needed.

"Come, our harvesting is done for the day. We have to do the rest of our chores now." Altair motions for Emil to come closer, to step away from the barn and the warm pool of chicken blood dripping from the work table and into the packed earth below.

Emil seems to weigh his options internally and takes a deep breath to steady himself. He nods and then takes another deep breath, his eyes lightening to their natural icy blue. "Y-yes," he says. He glances briefly at Markos, still standing uneasily with the ax clenched tight, yet lowered at least. Emil gives him a small wave and a tight smile, then follows Altair out of the gardens.

Altair's lessons with Henry almost always take the form of a lecture. Emil sits next to Henry in the living room of Number Five and attempts to pay attention but finds his mind wandering. Not because of any overwhelming sense to tear into someone's throat, but simply because the lecture is rather boring.

Somewhere in the hall, a clock chimes three o'clock. Emil can hear Mrs. Flint and Dawn in the kitchen making bread for the neighborhood. If he concentrates, he can hear snippets of their whispered conversation.

"I just don't know what to do with him sometimes, Mrs. Flint. He's growing so fast."

"Maybe Markos can help him with some magic? You know Markos would happily do it, if you asked."

"Oh, Mrs. Flint, you know Markos and I are just friends."

"Now," Altair is saying, motioning to a diagram with a long retractable pointer, "vampire fangs are often seen here and here, though sometimes they protrude from here or here, depending on the genetic makeup of the siring vampire."

Henry raises his hand. "What about your siring vampire?"

Altair grimaces. "We will not be discussing that at this lecture, but suffice it to say, he was a traditionally bred vampire."

Emil raises his hand. "What's an un-traditionally bred vampire?"

"A dhampir," responds Altair. "A vampire born from a mortal woman who has lain with a male vampire. They tend to be meeker, not so intent on indulging in bloodlust. Which is perhaps why they are a dying breed, so to speak."

"And there are fae vampires too, right?" asks Henry.

"Baobhan sith are considered vampiric in nature, yes," says Altair. "Now, as I was saying—"

"What's your favorite kind of blood?"

"B positive. Now—"

"What does cow's blood taste like?"

"Earthy. Now—"

"Can you eat actual food—"

"Occasionally, if it's something worth eating—"

"What—"

"Oh, for heaven's sake," mutters Altair,

slumping down in the chair. He abandons the pointer, his sigh as desolate as a king losing his empire to some indomitable foe.

The exaggerated sigh is what makes Emil laugh, though. Altair is shockingly easy to tease.

Altair shakes his head, ignoring the snickers from Emil and Henry, and buries his hands in his glossy black curls. Altair's hands are thin and graceful compared to Emil's, which are calloused from a youth spent working in the sun and certainly not helped by years of carrying a rifle on the battlefield.

His hands will always be like this, he realizes with some embarrassment, looking at his nobbly, pale fingers with chipped nails. He has no hope of ever earning the smooth, dexterous digits that Altair uses so expertly to button his sleeves or fix his tie. He thinks of the piano he had seen in the library of Number Two and, looking at Altair's hands right now, he can almost hear the music, knowing, just by looking at his fingers as they sink deeper into his hair, that Altair could play any song with envious expertise. Perhaps Emil will tease him into playing a song for him later this evening after they have their dinner.

"I'm sorry, Altair," he says. "We'll be quiet. Please, continue."

Altair eyes the two warily but grabs his pointer with a huff, using his free hand to straighten his hair. Henry stifles a snicker behind his hand, and Emil's lips flinch against the smile that is trying desperately to break through. But a stern look from Altair makes them school their expressions as best they can.

"As I was saying," Altair begins, angling his voice sternly at them, "vampire fangs are..."

"She clearly only wants him for his money," says Altair, his voice a little higher than it should be. "She is a strong, independent young woman, and she shouldn't shackle herself to the likes of...of...of a lying, manipulative—"

Book Club meetings are hosted on a rotation, and tonight's meeting falls to Mrs. Flint. They began the meeting in the sitting room, as appropriate, but have since migrated to the kitchen, where the platter of cucumber sandwiches and bite-sized cheesecakes resides. Emil hasn't read the book, but Altair seemed reluctant to leave him by himself, so he accompanied him next door to Number Three.

Number Three is a mirror of Number Two, but Mrs. Flint's decor sensibilities differ wildly from Altair's. Instead of rich mahogany and thick ornate rugs, Mrs. Flint has a surprisingly sparse decor theme, with birch wood floors and white cabinets set against white walls adorned with abstract paintings by Mrs. Flint herself. "I just dabble," she said humbly when he complimented the artist's skill.

Emil pops a cheesecake into his mouth and chews while listening to the debate. It's true, he realizes, that he can still eat solid foods if he so desires, but he finds that the act is satisfying only in its familiarity. The taste is comforting—a thick mix of cream and smooth chocolate that melts in his mouth—but beyond that, it is elementary, offering far less satisfaction than the crimson liquid he knows is waiting for him at home.

"Yes, Altair. I agree," says Dawn. "I just

think—"

"He was sort of dreamy, though," says Mrs. Flint.

Altair scoffs and mutters something under his breath.

"Oh, yes," says Arabella, "with those silver eyes and soft, scornful mouth, he just—"

"I don't really think the love interest is what we should be discussing. The author used some very inventive foreshadowing," begins Briar, opening his book and pointing to specific passages that he has underlined.

Emil smirks and sneaks a glance at Altair, who has leaned back in his chair, arms folded across his chest, with a look of annoyance.

"I agree with Altair," signs Markos. "The main character deserved more..."

Emil doesn't find the recipe in a book but written on a piece of parchment at the bottom of a drawer. It's a handwritten note, a translation of another piece of parchment that has long since been lost. Emil folds the paper into a square and stuffs it in his pocket.

Later, when Altair is absorbed in his

paperback, hand on his mouth in shock at a quip from the main love interest, Emil steps outside. He stands on the porch of Number Two, breathing in the smells of early night: the savory aroma of dinner being cooked, the light fragrance of bee balm in bloom, and the wet, mossy scent from the water-slicked cobblestones that line the fountain.

There is a rustle of leaves followed by a soft whistled bird call that comes from behind the bush between Number Two and Number Three.

"Mrs. Flint?" he asks quietly, darting a look at the closed door behind him to make sure that Altair hasn't heard him. "Is that you?"

A hoarse whisper answers him. "The hawk has landed."

"Mrs. Flint, this isn't necessary. I just wanted to ask you a favor and—"

"The hawk—"

"—has landed, yes." He sighs and runs his fingers through his hair. "The turtle is in the pond," he whispers back, impatiently.

Mrs. Flint pops her head up out of the bush. "Do you have it?"

He hands over the folded piece of

parchment. "You swear he will be able to eat some?"

She nods, reading through the recipe. "Vampires don't need food like the rest of us, but I've seen Altair sneak a few of my bite-size caramel cheesecakes and he's quite partial to a glass of my hackberry wine."

"And you think we can make the recipe for the next town meeting?"

"Oh yes, not a problem."

"Thanks, Mrs. Flint."

When Emil reenters Number Two, he stands in the main entryway, pausing to listen for Altair. He hears the rustle of paper turning, followed by a gasp and a muttered curse. He follows the sound into the library, where he sees Altair leaning forward in one of the chairs, his attention glued to the open book in front of him.

"Altair, could I ask you a favor?"

"Yes," he says distractedly, turning the page.

"Could you play me a song?" He motions toward the piano.

Altair looks up and blinks, looking from Emil to the piano, and then back again. "I suppose so. What would you like me to play?"

When Dawn, Markos, and Henry walk by
Number Two later that evening, they hear the
tentative sounds of a piano floating through
the open window and Emil saying, "No, not
quite like that. Here, like this."

Emil runs his fingers over the keys,
plucking out a jaunty tune and humming
along. Altair sits next to him on the piano
bench, their shoulders brushing against each
other.

"Hmm," says Altair. "You do the bass line
then, and I will come in with the melody."

Emil begins again, running his fingers
through a one-two-three rhythm, a stop-
and-go beat. Altair plucks a high note once,
then lets his fingers trickle down and up,
back and forth, the two concordant parts
melding together into a song that makes
Markos smile.

"I remember this song," he signs. "From
when I was young."

Dawn smiles too. "Perhaps we could
convince Altair and Emil to perform a recital
for us one day."

"That'd be cool," says Henry. "Do you

think they know anything by Metallica?"

Dawn turns to her son and links her arm with his. "Probably not, but maybe we can teach them?" she says conspiratorially. Then, quietly to Markos, she adds, "Something tells me that Altair would do it if Emil asked him to…"

Chapter 6

A left-hand glove for Markos.

A book for Dawn on healing potions from Altair's library.

A sharpened pair of pruning shears for Arabella, whose hair needs a trim.

This is what Emil has packed in the basket he is carrying to his first town meeting, which is being held in the courtyard. Mismatched chairs pulled from various houses are arranged in a circle by the fountain.

Briar and Markos have pulled out their fire pit and placed it in the center. Henry leans over the logs, attempting to start a fire by snapping his fingers and calling a flame from the ether. Although he gets most of his magic from his mother's side, his father, as unknown as he is to Henry, will have given him a particular affinity for flame.

"Almost," signs Markos. "Think of the color of fire. Deep red and cool blue. Think of how the sun feels against your skin."

Henry nods and narrows his eyes as he stares intently at his hand. And then, with a small grunt, he snaps his fingers, and a spark appears in between. He snaps his fingers again, and the spark catches alight. His face brightens, and he lets the flame tumble between his fingers like sand. It lands on the logs and spreads quickly.

With the fire starting and the sun just beginning to set, there is a glow around the courtyard that makes Emil smile. It's been four weeks since his unexpected arrival at Griffinwood Close and two weeks since he began his life as a vampire—or, as Altair calls it, with a hint of fondness, his interminable damnation.

If this is damnation, he thinks, looking around the courtyard, then perhaps his mother's religion had it all wrong.

Tomorrow morning, he will meet with Briar, Markos, and Henry for their now-daily early morning run. He enjoys the strength he finds in his muscles now and the weight of the cold morning air in his lungs. It makes him feel more alive than when he had a heartbeat.

He has been learning more of Markos's signs and is becoming more fluent with each conversation.

He has also been welcomed into the Griffinwood Book Club. Next week, they will meet to discuss a classic from Dawn's time, a romance story about teen vampires that both annoyed and ensnared him.

Altair would never admit it, but he, too, was engrossed in the story and stayed up an entire night to finish the book. Emil could hear his muttered reactions through the wall well into the next morning.

Emil has become quite adept at knowing where Altair is in relation to himself. He can feel the space between them like a physical entity pressing against his side. At first, the farther Altair was, the more Emil feared succumbing to the tightness in his gums and the hollowness in his belly telling him lies. He would become dizzy with the need to sink his teeth into something soft and fleshy until Altair was standing next to him, his hand on his arm in silent reassurance.

Now, as Emil looks at Altair from across

the fire, he feels the space between them as more of a gentle tether, as if they are joined by a rope from chest to chest. His silent heart feels full of warmth for Altair.

Altair settles in the chair beside Emil and hands him a glass of Mrs. Flynn's homemade wine. "It's not blood, but it'll take the edge off until our proper meal after the meeting."

Emil takes the glass with a grateful smile, his pale fingers brushing lightly against Altair's dark skin. He can feel the coolness of Altair's silver signet ring, and it reminds him of Valentine's necklace, hidden in the pillowcase in his room.

He's not sure why he has kept the necklace a secret, except for the fact that it reminds him of his attack and of the horrors he witnessed as he was forced to slay those monsters who ambushed him and his fellow soldiers in the middle of the forest.

Altair had told him that the monster who gave him his cursed bite was a former lover who tore him asunder, limb from limb, for months before Altair was able to escape, stumbling like a newborn lamb until he found himself face-to-face with Arabella Twigs, who had been quite startled by the yellow-eyed vampire, disheveled and covered in layers of dried, crusty blood.

Mrs. Flint had already been settled into Number Three, and soon after Altair arrived, Briar and Markos stumbled up on the Close together—two wayward souls brought together in the depths of the wilderness and led toward the Close by helpful trees.

Then came Dawn and her half-demon son, Henry (who may or may not be the Antichrist; she confided in him a week ago as they sat sipping elderflower liqueur on the porch of Number Five).

Although they are all different—from different places, dimensions, times, and cultures—they are joined here, in the middle of the cobblestone courtyard, by their pasts, linked irrevocably by trauma, estrangement, and, in some cases, the deaths they have caused along the way.

As Emil listens to Henry recite an essay about thermodynamics in magical practice, set by Markos a few weeks ago, he realizes what else everyone here has in common: a need for family and connection.

A need for acceptance, he adds to himself.

Although he is still very much a newcomer,

Chapter 7

ut on Dawn's hand is not as bad as it
 and Henry leaves to fetch the first
t. Dawn apologizes profusely as Briar
 her a cloth napkin.

air knows that Emil has removed
lf from the courtyard. He felt the
f his presence as sure as a fire being
guished.

rkos catches Altair's eye and signs, "I
 he went toward the barn."

ll go find him," he says. "Thank you,
os."

 Altair leaves the warmth of the
ard, he feels a sense of panic rising in
roat, and he flexes his hands, worried,
e first time, that he may have to do
 than snap Emil's neck.

d yet, when Altair does find Emil, he is

he feels the sweetness of affection in his
chest, so different from the fire of hunger he
felt when he first arrived but equally strong
in conviction.

Mrs. Flint announces her next pick for
Book Club, and Altair confirms that he has
a copy of the title and that he will pass it
along to Dawn tomorrow so that she may
begin replicating the text using a highly
modified illusion spell she developed with
Markos. Briar shares that this year's Summer
Solstice play will be a somewhat condensed
adaptation of *As You Like It*.

There is a collective groan at this news,
as they all remember the disaster that was
Romeo and Juliet from a previous season.
"We will triple-check the swords this time, I
assure you," he says.

"And, of course, we would like to thank our
new neighbor, Emil, for selecting our treat
for tonight, a delicacy from... well, a faraway
place indeed." She leans close to Altair and
says, only to him, "You might want to sample
this one, Altair."

The town meeting concludes, and the
residents of Griffinwood Close linger close
to the fire, allowing the night breeze and

the stars to lull them into a mellow sort of gathering, their wine-tinged lips easily laughing and conversing.

Emil stays seated, content, and heavy-lidded. The wine has indeed helped ease the hunger, and he finds himself reluctant to stand, preferring instead to watch the group, their silhouettes honey-lined with light from the fire. He watches as Altair sniffs suspiciously at the platter of deep-fried dough drenched in honey and colored yellow with saffron.

Altair looks startled and turns around, his amber eyes searching for Emil. When their eyes meet, Altair gives him a wild, confused look and opens his mouth. But he doesn't seem to find the words he's looking for because he closes his mouth with a bemused smile and a shake of his head. He uses one of Markos's signs to say "thank you" before popping the treat into his mouth. His eyes close instantly, and he is lost in a moment he thought he had forgotten.

But then a glass shatters, and with it, the comforting blanket of the night is ripped from Emil's shoulders as the smell of blood fills the air.

Emil knows wh
remembers the lil
extra something th
tight and uncomfor

Dawn is holding
glass at her feet.
saying. "It was an a

It is with a sh
realizes he has tak
his mouth open in
breath and closes l
walks away.

The
looks
aid l
passe

Al
hims
lack
extin

M
think

"I
Mark

As
court
his tl
for tl
more

Ar

bent over a goat, and the smell of blood mixes with dry hay. They will lose a goat, which is hardly a sacrifice when the alternative is the loss of a neighbor. He feels unabashedly proud of Emil for making this decision despite the monstrous irrationality that must be raging in his veins.

Altair kneels down next to Emil and places a hand on his shoulder, whispering his name as he does so. Emil looks up, his eyes as red as the blood that covers his mouth, which has dripped down and stained the front of his shirt—the blood that could have very well belonged to Dawn if Emil hadn't the wherewithal to remove himself and change the focus of his intent.

"I'm so sorry, I'm so..." says Emil, tears mixing with the blood that coats his skin.

Altair nods. "Let's get you cleaned up."

He helps Emil stand and then throws his suit jacket over his shoulders, as much to quell the sudden shivering in Emil's limbs as to potentially hide the gruesome sight from their neighbors as they pass through the courtyard and slip quietly into Number Two.

Altair leads Emil up the stairs and into the bathroom with its chipped sink and speckled mirror. Altair has no real use for the bathroom besides basic bathing, and so the room is sparse, with only a comb resting on the counter to prove it's been in use. Altair lowers Emil to the ledge of the bathtub, leaning beyond him to turn on the tap. He removes the jacket from Emil's shoulders and unbuttons the shirt beneath, his fingers brushing against Emil's chest. Emil shivers against the touch, his hands clenching and unclenching.

Dipping a washcloth into the warm water in the bath, Altair brings it up to Emil's face and gently wipes away the blood. The water drips down Emil's chest, and it mixes with the blood as it travels down his torso, turning his skin pink.

"I'm sorry," says Emil, his head swimming with wine and blood. "That you have to...to do this."

Altair shakes his head. "There is nothing to be sorry about."

"Can you tell me about him? About Valentine? Why would he do this to me?"

"I don't know," says Altair hoarsely. "But Valentine isn't one for thinking ahead."

"So you don't think he will be able to find

he feels the sweetness of affection in his chest, so different from the fire of hunger he felt when he first arrived but equally strong in conviction.

Mrs. Flint announces her next pick for Book Club, and Altair confirms that he has a copy of the title and that he will pass it along to Dawn tomorrow so that she may begin replicating the text using a highly modified illusion spell she developed with Markos. Briar shares that this year's Summer Solstice play will be a somewhat condensed adaptation of *As You Like It*.

There is a collective groan at this news, as they all remember the disaster that was Romeo and Juliet from a previous season. "We will triple-check the swords this time, I assure you," he says.

"And, of course, we would like to thank our new neighbor, Emil, for selecting our treat for tonight, a delicacy from... well, a faraway place indeed." She leans close to Altair and says, only to him, "You might want to sample this one, Altair."

The town meeting concludes, and the residents of Griffinwood Close linger close to the fire, allowing the night breeze and the stars to lull them into a mellow sort of gathering, their wine-tinged lips easily laughing and conversing.

Emil stays seated, content, and heavy-lidded. The wine has indeed helped ease the hunger, and he finds himself reluctant to stand, preferring instead to watch the group, their silhouettes honey-lined with light from the fire. He watches as Altair sniffs suspiciously at the platter of deep-fried dough drenched in honey and colored yellow with saffron.

Altair looks startled and turns around, his amber eyes searching for Emil. When their eyes meet, Altair gives him a wild, confused look and opens his mouth. But he doesn't seem to find the words he's looking for because he closes his mouth with a bemused smile and a shake of his head. He uses one of Markos's signs to say "thank you" before popping the treat into his mouth. His eyes close instantly, and he is lost in a moment he thought he had forgotten.

But then a glass shatters, and with it, the comforting blanket of the night is ripped from Emil's shoulders as the smell of blood fills the air.

Emil knows who it is immediately; he remembers the lilacs and honey and that extra something that makes his gums feel tight and uncomfortable.

Dawn is holding her hand, a broken wine glass at her feet. "I'm so sorry," she is saying. "It was an accident."

It is with a shock of horror that Emil realizes he has taken a step closer to her, his mouth open in a snarl. He takes a deep breath and closes his eyes, then turns and walks away.

Chapter 7

The cut on Dawn's hand is not as bad as it looks, and Henry leaves to fetch the first aid kit. Dawn apologizes profusely as Briar passes her a cloth napkin.

Altair knows that Emil has removed himself from the courtyard. He felt the lack of his presence as sure as a fire being extinguished.

Markos catches Altair's eye and signs, "I think he went toward the barn."

"I'll go find him," he says. "Thank you, Markos."

As Altair leaves the warmth of the courtyard, he feels a sense of panic rising in his throat, and he flexes his hands, worried, for the first time, that he may have to do more than snap Emil's neck.

And yet, when Altair does find Emil, he is

me? That he's using me to get to you?"

"I don't know," he says again. "I do know that you are meant to be here. The Close would not reveal itself to you without gleaning something honorable and worthwhile inside of your heart." He pauses, and when he speaks again, the words seem to tumble from his mouth. "Valentine was beautiful once, and I loved him for it. But he wanted nothing but blood. Was mad with wanting. I was too, for a time. I'm not proud of it, Emil, but I've killed and feasted. I sat next to him and watched while he did the same. Until I made a decision he didn't like and then he turned his malevolence on me. Love born from violence always ends with violence."

"Do you still love him?"

"No," says Altair, gently but with enough force that Emil finds himself looking right into Altair's eyes, trying hard to show him that he's glad of that. He wants to say something about love and fate and hackberry wine. He wants to describe the feeling growing in his chest, right behind his sternum, when he thinks about Altair. He wants to whisper something into Altair's ear, not because he has anything particular to say but because the skin looks soft and his lips are burning.

Altair's eyes flicker down to Emil's parted lips, and for a brief second, he, too, looks like he wants to whisper something—anything—against Emil's mouth.

Emil moves first, grabbing Altair's free hand and pressing a kiss to his knuckles. "Thank you," he says against Altair's skin, the silver signet ring cold against his lips. "I would never be able to do this without you, Altair."

Altair scoffs. "You're stronger than you realize, my dear Emil. I know of very few younglings who would make as rational a decision as you made tonight."

It is Emil's turn to scoff, and he averts his eyes, waving off Altair's compliment. Altair catches his chin in his hand and turns his face back to his, saying, "No, I mean it." Then he leans back, his eyes glittering gold in the low light of the bathroom. "You will make a respectable vampire yet," he says with a smirk.

"That is all I desire," says Emil, returning the smirk.

Part 3

Summer

Chapter 8

As Spring falls to the reins of Summer, the residents of Griffinwood Close all but abandon their homes, enjoying the few months of unwavering heat before the inevitable drop toward Winter.

Meals are consumed on front porches and back patios. Books are read in the field next to the orchard, far away from dark, stifling sitting rooms. Markos and Briar make shaved ice flavored with crushed fruit, while Mrs. Flint makes lemonade spiked with moonshine. Henry sneaks some at one of the town meetings and regrets his decision the next morning.

The flock of pixies steals some lemonade too, and they swirl about the courtyard, leaving a trail of half-consumed rotting fruit and rainbow glitter on each doorstep.

The fountain seems to grow, inch by inch, until it is a swimming pool, and Arabella spends her evenings with her feet in the shallow side, watching Markos do laps around the perimeter.

It is soon revealed that Emil does not know how to swim, so Altair reluctantly adds swimming to their daily itinerary. Markos graciously takes over swimming lessons when it is revealed that Altair, in his old age, has forgotten how to swim. Henry joins in, and they spend more time laughing at Emil's feeble attempts than instructing. At some point, Emil challenges them to see how long they can each hold their breath underwater.

Emil wins due to the fact that he doesn't technically need to breathe anymore.

Briar decides to put on a one-faun synchronized swimming recital, and halfway through Summer, they gather in the courtyard to enjoy the performance, their spirits lifted by the evening breeze.

Altair reads by the pool, having pulled his comfiest reading chair out of the library. At some point, he moves from the chair to the side of the pool, removing his shoes and rolling up his trousers to enjoy the cool water on his feet. He sits next to Arabella, holding his book up high with both of his hands to prevent the accidental drowning of the valuable collector's edition.

"You know, when I was young, just a root really, I spent a summer in love," says Arabella one evening.

Altair gives her a sidelong look, lightly concealed surprise in his expression. Arabella rarely shares such information willingly.

She smiles at the memory, twisting her walnut necklace around her fingers. "My father didn't approve, and I let him talk me out of marriage. A thing I have regretted every day since."

"It is an easy thing," says Altair, "to be bandied about by external forces. Much easier than moving with purpose against the tide."

"Indeed," she says, looking up at him. "I wonder, sometimes, if secluding ourselves here is really just us letting ourselves be bandied about. We certainly aren't moving with purpose, are we? We aren't moving at all, really."

"Life here can feel stagnant, I suppose. But do not forget that we have all removed ourselves from a fate much worse than stagnation. We are rebuilding ourselves even as we take comfort in routine and simplicity."

Arabella's rose petals look luminescent in the fading daylight when she looks over at him. "You are quite the philosopher, my dear Altair. I am grateful to have you here."

"I am grateful to be here," he says.

She looks out at the fountain and at their neighbors laughing at some shared joke, and she smiles. "I'm happy Emil is here too. Aren't you?"

"Yes, indeed. I'm happy you're all here. I am eternally grateful for all of our neighbors," he says.

She glances back at Altair to see that he is looking toward the opposite side of the fountain, though there is a wisp of a smile on his lips that makes her think he is looking at one neighbor in particular.

Emil screams, thrashing against his sheets until he finds himself on the floor, kicking against the remnants of a dream.

He takes a deep, shaky breath and closes his eyes. He can hear Altair moving in the room next door, a rustle of fabric, the soft thud as he sits his book down.

The door to Emil's room opens, the light from the hallway blinding him briefly until it is blocked by Altair leaning down to peer at Emil's face. Emil feels Altair's hands on his shoulders, but he shakes them off. "I'm fine," he mumbles.

He takes another shuddering breath as he pushes himself into a sitting position, his back against the bed. "I'm sorry to wake you."

Altair hides his concern well as he sits next to Emil, his hands folded in his lap. "I wasn't sleeping," he says. "I'm trying to finish that book before our next meeting."

"How are you liking it?"

He shrugs. "It's fine."

There is a pause as Emil takes another shaky breath, brushing his hair back from his forehead.

"What was it about? Your nightmare...?" asks Altair, quietly.

Emil hesitates. "It was...Valentine."

Altair makes a noncommittal hum, his attention quite suddenly enraptured by a piece of lint on his burgundy robe.

"It was when he...when he bit me," continues Emil.

Altair nods knowingly and looks up at Emil. The false moonlight from the window behind him frames his hair like a halo, turning Altair into some benevolent celestial, constellations in the soft curve of his mouth, in the twinkle of understanding in his eye. "Would you like to talk about it?"

Emil shakes his head. "It was just a dream. More of an impression, really. Just, the smell of him, the fear. I could...I could feel the sweat trickling down my cheek, the feeling of his...his teeth...he said something, in the dream. He said, 'I'm coming for you little rabbit.'" Emil's face crumples in fear. "Does that mean—? Can he—?"

Altair places a hand on Emil's thigh. The warmth of his touch feels like sunshine. "It was just a dream."

"Can I ask you a question?"

"Of course."

"What exactly happened between you two?"

He sighs, removing his hand from Emil's thigh to run it through his hair. Emil misses the warmth immediately but waits patiently as Altair searches for the correct words.

"He killed someone I had become fond of," he says eventually. "A female vampire. It wasn't romantic, but Valentine wouldn't listen and he was nothing if not thorough. I could only identify her because of a necklace I had gifted her. A gold locket. Valentine stole it from her burning corpse and wore it proudly. I will never forgive him for that."

"A gold locket?"

"Hmm, yes. It had my family crest on it. An asp twisting around the sun."

Emil thinks briefly of the stolen locket hiding in his pillowcase and knows he should say something, but can't bring himself to disturb the companionable silence that has fallen between them. Altair is right, he reassures himself, it was just a dream. He will tell Altair about the locket later.

When he does feel brave enough to speak, he nods toward the book on his nightstand. "It's quite awful, isn't it?"

"It's horrid," says Altair, then adds, somewhat sheepishly, "I'm enjoying it immensely."

Chapter 9

Opening day for the Summer Solstice play arrives. As usual, they have sent out their long-standing invitation to the play's creator, a Mr. William Shakespeare, trusting that Griffinwood's defenses would part for such an important person.

Their invitation goes unanswered, but they press on regardless, enlisting the skills of Mrs. Flint to paint the backdrop and utilizing Emil's youngling strength to install the scenery and reinforce the wood platform set up in the middle of the courtyard.

The swords are tested three times and eventually given the all-clear by Altair.

The sun begins its slow descent toward the horizon, and the audience settles into their chairs, snacks and glasses of wine in hand. There is a hushed moment of silence, and then the curtains open to reveal Briar, dressed in his best waistcoat and red bowtie.

"My esteemed neighbors, I thank you all for attending our annual Summer Solstice play," he says. "Without further ado, I implore you to enjoy Griffinwood Players's...somewhat abbreviated...adaptation of Shakespeare's *As You Like It*."

As the first act begins, Emil realizes that "somewhat abbreviated" is a bit of an understatement, and he quickly finds himself lost as they skip over entire sections of action, summarizing large portions with a few sentences directed toward the audience. Additionally, all of the characters are played by the same three people (Markos, Dawn, and Arabella), which leads to a great deal of confusion as to who is portraying whom.

Arabella has just appeared on stage wearing part of her costume for Orlando and part of her costume for Silvius.

"Altair," he whispers, "who is that again?"

Altair moves close to Emil, and he stays there, leaning against his shoulder, as he explains the play in a hushed voice.

Emil listens intently but inevitably falls to distraction, his skin prickling at the rumble of Altair's voice against his ear. A lock of Altair's hair falls carelessly over his forehead, and Emil tightens his fist against the urge to brush it back into place.

This is the closest they've been since that cool Spring night, sitting next to each other on the edge of the tub, Emil shaking with regret and Altair's hand on his cheek in reassurance. Altair's voice is just as strong, just as warm in his ear tonight, and Emil takes a look at him, startled to see that Altair's gaze is on him and not the stage.

Emil smiles lazily and parts his lips, his canine teeth still youthfully sharp. Altair turns his head to the side in silent entreaty, a ghost of something quite like hunger in his eyes.

But then Arabella's voice resounds, and Altair's gaze is torn from the heat of Emil to Orlando, asking, "Is't possible that on so little acquaintance you should like her? That, but seeing, you should love her?"

Chapter 10

There is one particular book club meeting that gets rather heated.

A vote is taken at the subsequent town meeting and it is decided that it shall never be discussed again.

Part 4

Autumn

Chapter 11

The days stretch on, and Emil takes comfort in their routine, rising early to run with Markos and Briar, working diligently on a glove for Markos, and interrupting Henry's lectures with silly questions.

The end of the month draws near, and the residents of Griffinwood Close gather in the courtyard for Henry's fourteenth birthday. Mrs. Flint makes a birthday cake, and they sing a song in Henry's honor as he blows out the candles. They share the cake after dinner, the flock of pixies dancing around the courtyard as they steal mouthfuls of icing, their glittery trails leaving a fine dust on everything they pass over.

Altair agrees to perform a song at Henry's request, and so the piano is carried out of the library at Number Two and placed next to the fountain. When he begins the first few bars of a song from Henry's childhood, Henry sulks around for a few beats, complaining that it doesn't sound quite the same when translated to a piano. He ends up dancing anyway, twirling his mother around with a laugh and learning some choreography from Briar. At one point, he extends his wings and does a few loops in the air, landing on the top of the fountain to applause.

The piano is charmed to continue playing while Altair returns to his chair next to Emil. Emil leans back, stretching his long legs out in front of him. His eyes crinkle at Arabella's unconventional dance moves, and he sips on a glass of Mrs. Flint's hackberry wine.

It takes him some moments to realize that Altair is looking at him, scrutinizing his face with the same narrow focus Altair applies to all challenges with which he is forced to reckon. Emil smirks as he takes a sip. "Like what you see?" he asks recklessly.

He realizes giddily that the wine has gone to his head. Interminably damned or not, there is no preventing drunkenness when it comes to Mrs. Flint's homemade hackberry wine.

Altair seems taken aback by the forwardness in Emil's voice but finds himself contemplating the question regardless, cocking his head to the side and appreciating the long, angular lines of Emil's visage.

As the flock of pixies flies overhead, drops of glitter sprinkle down to land on Emil's cheeks, and Altair finally admits to himself that the peace and quiet with which he has been so preoccupied pales in comparison to life with Emil, which is vibrant, filled with laughter and smiles, and wine-soaked, humorous conversations that wind and twist and turn back on themselves until Altair is sure they have discussed everything under the sun, moon, and stars in several different universes.

Emil has grown a lot in the past months, taking on the mantle of interminable damnation with aplomb. And further still, Emil's presence has deepened Altair's connection to his neighbors.

Last Wednesday, while having lunch at Number Four, Briar told Altair that he had never seen him with such a wide smile before, a comment that made Altair stutter a bit before he could get out a startled "Thank you."

Similarly, Dawn commented a few days ago, as they sat on the back porch of Number Five surrounded by hydrangeas in full bloom, that she likes it when Altair and Emil come around for a glass of wine after dinner. "I think Henry enjoys having Emil around," she said. "They get along remarkably well."

Arabella, too, has enjoyed Altair and Emil's visits to her conservatory, and she has become quite fond of Altair's stories of the desert and a time long lost to the same erosion the ancient temples he describes have surely suffered.

Altair realizes that Emil is still looking at him, awaiting an answer to his question with parted lips and eyes full of some unreadable, distant emotion.

However, Altair never gets the chance to respond. There is a loud boom that echoes around the courtyard, stealing whatever words were about to pass his lips. The sound bounces off the griffin sculpture that crowns the fountain, and the sculpture cracks, a wing sliding down to the ground.

A second sound rumbles beneath them as if a mountain god has stamped his foot down in anger. A crackling sound of lightning striking the entryway of Griffinwood Close draws their attention to the wrought-iron structure and the hooded figure that stands beneath it.

Chapter 12

There is panic in everyone's eyes, even Arabella's. The figure lowers their hood to reveal blond hair and tar-black eyes. Two hellhounds stand next to him, snapping their teeth at an invisible enemy.

"It's him," whispers Altair. "It's Valentine."

Valentine cocks his head to the side, his eyes darting back and forth as if searching for Altair in the dark. "Altair," he says quietly. "I know you're there, darling. Won't you come out to play?"

"The defenses hold," says Arabella, reassuringly. "He can't see us."

"Henry," says Dawn quietly, as one of the hounds sniffs the air and then growls, low and deep, in their direction. "Go back home, go down to the basement, and lock the door."

Henry shakes his head, his wings extending outward. "I can help," he says, snapping his fingers to form a ball of fire in the palm of his hand.

"Henry, listen to your mother," says Altair. "All of you should go."

"Altair, we can't leave you—" begins Briar.

"You can. This is my fight."

"Mine, too," adds Emil.

Altair glances at him briefly, but Valentine speaks again.

"Did you find my little rabbit? He took something from me."

Emil's throat bobs in fear, and he can feel Altair's gaze, as hot as the fire still in Henry's palm.

"What does he mean?" he asks quietly.

Emil avoids his gaze for a beat, then looks up, his crystal blue eyes meeting Altair's amber gaze. "I took a necklace."

Altair's look is unreadable. "Go get it," he says harshly, before turning back to Valentine.

"I can smell you, Altair," Valentine says, looking back and forth, his eyes sweeping over some view that is unknown to those inside Griffinwood Close. Altair wonders what Valentine sees. An empty field? Darkness? He hasn't left the Close since he arrived, and he's not sure what it looks like on the other side of the gate.

Valentine looks the same as Altair remembers, though his eyes are blacker, the pupils bleeding outward like ink dropped in water. His blond hair is tied back from his face, which is all sharp angles and pale skin. His full lips are still covered in last night's meal. The hellhounds are new, he thinks, and he wonders what deal Valentine made to garner the loyalty of the two fiendish creatures.

When Emil returns, it is with a gold locket, and Altair feels dizzy because he recognizes the necklace, and knows the lines of the etching, the asp circled around the sun as it rises from the horizon. He knows it as well as he knows his own hands.

He loved the woman who once wore the locket and considered her a sister until Valentine stole the pendant from her neck. And now Valentine stands in front of his home with blood-dipped fingernails and teeth as sharp as a knife.

No wonder he found Griffinwood, he thinks.

Altair takes the locket from Emil and looks up at his neighbors, his heart bursting with fear for them.

Valentine reaches forward with a long nail, and there is a scratching sound, like a knife on metal, and the sky overhead cracks. It sounds like lightning at first, but the clouds above are gone, and the sky is a black veil of nothingness.

"What are we going to do?" asks Mrs. Flint. She looks nervously back at home. "I can...I can always go get my cap—"

Altair stuffs the locket into the pocket of his waistcoat, resigned to his fate, wondering if Valentine's blood will taste as vile as the vampire himself. "That won't be necessary, Mrs. Flint. You are all going to retire to your homes. I will take care of our unexpected intruder."

"Wait," says Emil. He looks at Altair with sadness in his eyes and reaches out to touch his cheek. The touch is so brief that it feels like a breeze brushing against his skin. Then, with swift and sure movements, Emil reaches into Altair's pocket to grab the locket.

He turns and runs headlong through the gates.

The Griffinwood defenses clamp down immediately, and before Altair can do anything but step forward, night descends upon the courtyard so thickly that it creates an impenetrable curtain, blocking the courtyard from whatever is happening beyond. There is a scratch of metal as the bronze griffin rights itself, unbalanced as it is, and shuffles to the entrance, blocking the gate from anyone who may be coming or going.

Altair shouts, though he is not sure what words come out. He simply shouts, beating a fist upon the griffin until the smell of his blood lingers in the cool Autumn air, until he feels a dull throb in his hand and is sure the bones must be crushed.

Yet the statue stands immovable, deaf to Altair's demands.

So Altair moves to the side, where the impenetrable curtain of darkness separates him from whatever is beyond. He presses his palm against the nothingness as if he can will it to dissolve. He is unaware of what is happening behind him and doesn't notice that his neighbors have set up chairs and dragged mattresses out so that they can watch the gate.

An hour passes, and Altair stands still, his spine stiff as the bronze griffin statue, still barring the way out. He needs to eat, but he has forgotten how to move.

At some point, a glass of blood is pressed into his hand, and he sips it, unwilling to take his eyes away from the darkness, as if he can pierce the nothingness with sight alone. If only he keeps looking, it will part for him, and he will be able to kill the past that looms over him.

It should be me, he thinks. Emil belongs here, and, for the first time since he arrived, Altair doesn't want to stay at the Close—not without Emil.

Altair presses his palm against the darkness again, praying silently to the spell that holds this place together.

Let me find him. Let me bring him home. Let me replace him in this fight.

But the spell holds strong, impassive to his pleading.

At some point, he is eased into a chair by someone, but his limbs ache with worry, and he jumps up moments later. He paces back and forth. He will wear a divot in the stones, a cut through the ground beneath him as deep as a grave.

He does not care.

When his body finally succumbs to its limitations and Altair slumps into a chair, the sun has just begun to rise, casting the courtyard in a rosy glow that would normally be pleasant and hopeful but instead reminds him of a stain of blood that cannot be washed from a strip of fabric.

It's Markos who notices the darkness thinning at first. He stands up quickly, moving toward the impenetrable veil and pointing. "It's him," he signs. "It's Emil."

They watch as the darkness lifts and Emil stumbles forward. There is blood on his face, dripping down his mouth, coating the front of his shirt, and staining his hands. His eyes are blood–red and unfocused. Behind him, collapsed by the entryway, is the bloodied corpse of Valentine, his two hellhounds nowhere to be seen.

Altair wonders vaguely how Emil is still standing. He was sure Valentine's years would have made him more than a worthy adversary, but perhaps there is more strength in a youngling vampire than Altair remembered. Perhaps Valentine had met his end at the hands of a monster he sought to create and use as a weapon. How fitting, he thinks dumbly.

Emil stumbles forward, his red eyes fading to a deep mazarine blue. When Altair grabs his shoulders to steady him, Emil looks up and leans into the embrace, his hands braced on each side of Altair's waist.

"You stupid, foolish..." Altair begins.

Emil's mouth quirks sideways in some wild, feral emotion. He holds out his hand to cup Altair's chin, brushing his thumb lightly against Altair's bottom lip. "It was worth it," he says, so quietly that Altair wonders if he's the only one who hears it.

Part 5

Winter

Chapter 13

The griffin sits proudly on its pillar, wings held aloft as if readying to take flight.

Snowflakes land on the bronze and immediately melt, as if the sculpture were more than just metal but bones and flesh blessed with the warmth of life.

There is a large line on its wing where it had been put back together, welded complete by Markos and Henry, who have taken an interest in metalsmithing. The statue wears a knitted scarf from Mrs. Flint along with a cap from Briar's collection. Tinsel hangs from the griffin's beak.

The fountain it sits upon is frozen, but it has expanded to become a decently sized ice rink. Markos is teaching Dawn to skate in the distance, their laughter echoing around the courtyard.

"How about here?" asks Emil. He holds a tree upright and absentmindedly scratches at the scar below his eye. The scar is the only evidence of his fight with Valentine. Emil knows that he was lucky—that his years as a soldier coupled with his youngling rage gave him the edge he needed to overcome Valentine's strength and malevolence, and that without love and fear for his neighbors fueling the fire in his limbs, he would not have walked away from the fight at all.

Briar looks at the tree, angling his head in thought. "That's a little too close to the fountain, I think. Maybe a little more to the right?"

Emil sighs and lifts the tree, shifting it down a foot in the requested direction.

"Hmm..." begins Briar. "I just don't..."

Emil groans, shaking his head. He looks over at Altair, who is perched next to Arabella on the side of the frozen fountain, reading a book. "Altair, what do you think?"

Altair looks up. "I think it's perfect right there, my dear."

"I do too," says Arabella.

Briar all but tosses his hands in the air as he mumbles vaguely that the "tree is still not quite centered," though he seems unable to communicate what landmarks the tree should be centered between.

The snow seems to lessen and eventually stop altogether as the residents of Griffinwood Close gather together to decorate the tree with tinsel, strings of lights, glossy baubles and handmade clay ornaments, garlands of dried cranberries and slices of oranges, and delicately wrapped candies made by Briar.

Mrs. Flint's mulled wine is brought out in a large simmering cauldron. Dawn sees Henry sneaking a sip or two but pretends not to, smirking a little at his grimace after a particularly large gulp.

Briar and Markos bring out their firepit, and Henry snaps a flame into existence. Arabella has knitted everyone matching sweaters, which they wear under thick wool coats and long striped scarves.

As day turns into night, the snow picks up again, as if encouraged by their revelry and cheery smiles. Red noses and cheeks are ignored in favor of spending more time in each other's company, refilling glasses with wine and plates with roast chicken and sweet potatoes, with a heaping spoonful of holiday pie on the side.

With a wave and wiggle of her wand, Dawn enchants a few candles to float around them, and, as one floats by Emil, Altair comes to stand beside him, his hands stuffed in the pockets of his coat despite the fact that he is far from cold.

"I know we are meant to exchange presents in the morning, my dear Emil, but I have something I would like to give you now, if you will indulge me." He pulls a small box out of his pocket.

"I already have everything I need, Altair," he says.

"Still," Altair replies, holding the box out to him, "I would like you to have this."

The box is small and velvety, and when Emil snaps it open, he finds a silver signet ring that matches the one adorning Altair's finger.

"I had Markos and Henry make it for me. I...I would like it very much if..."

"Yes," says Emil, slipping the ring on his finger and then reaching for Altair's hand. He mumbles "Always" before leaning forward to press his lips against Altair's cheek.

When he pulls away, however, Altair

catches his face and presses a kiss to his lips instead, drawing him closer with a hand on his lower back. Emil smiles against the kiss, lips soft and tasting of berries. His hand is on Altair's neck, and he fingers one of the black curls that rest against his shirt collar. Emil laughs against Altair's lips, and when the kiss ends, he is reluctant to let him go. "Altair, I do believe I have fallen in love with you."

"An easy mistake to make," replies Altair with a smirk. "I find that I am quite in love with you as well, my dear Emil."

Fingers still interlaced, they look upon their friends, who are in the midst of a rousing rendition of a traditional yuletide carol from Briar's culture—a bittersweet story about a snowflake falling in love with a bonfire.

Altair and Emil, dizzy with wine and love, join in, and their voices unite as the song floats upward into the sky, with the smoke from the fire and the snow flurries and the flock of pixies who are, as usual, drunk on Mrs. Flint's mulled wine.

A *Letter to*
William Shakespeare

Dear William,

It is hard to believe that an entire year has passed since our last correspondence, but, alas, here we are!

I am once again writing to extend a most loving invitation to Griffinwood Players' adaptation of your masterpiece *As You Like It*.

I would like to assure you that our safety precautions have been amplified in this production to prevent another Romeo incident. Indeed, we have triple-checked the swords this time, so you have nothing to fear!

It is perfectly safe!

Curtains are at six o'clock in the evening. Refreshments will be made available.

Mrs. Flint has been keeping a few bottles of her rather tasty hackberry wine for just this occasion. Markos, however, would like me to remind you that Mrs. Flint's hackberry wine can induce drunkenness in even the most solid of constitutions and he implores you to consider your accommodations to and fro.

Arabella would like to reassure you that, should you succumb to the refreshments, you are more than welcome to utilize her spare bedroom, provided that you are amenable to sleeping on a bed of leaves.

Altair says hello, as usual, and his partner, Emil, would like you to know that he is looking forward to meeting you. Emil is new to the Close, but he is a welcome addition. I think you'll like him immensely.

Originally, Altair and Emil were residing in Number Two, but they have since moved into Number Six, which is much more suitable for a couple and can accommodate a much larger selection of books—in fact, Altair was wondering if you could bring a few titles with you? His current collection is somewhat stagnant. Regardless, Number Six has the nicest sitting room and a lovely veranda, and we are all happy to see Altair settled with such a fine young man. Now, if only Markos will admit his feelings for a certain redhead!

But I digress.

Dawn sends her love, and Henry has a question he would like to ask you for a research paper he is writing: when and why did you start writing?

I do hope you are able to attend!

Yours truly,

Briar Michael Fernbug

About the Author

J. LYNN CARR may be a newly published author, but she has been writing for many years; it just took her a very long time to finish something. Before writing, her main creative outlet was painting, and she still considers it a significant part of her life.

Carr resides in Austin, TX, with her husband and their two beloved dogs, Milly and Freddie.

9 7989 88 208464